Bear Wants More

Karma Wilson

illustrations by Jane Chapman

MARGARET K. McELDERRY BOOKS

New York   London   Toronto   Sydney   Singapore

visit us at www.abdopublishing.com

Reinforced library bound edition published in 2009 by Spotlight, a division of ABDO Publishing Group, 8000 West 78th Street, Edina, Minnesota 55439. This edition was reprinted with permission of Margaret K. McElderry Books, an imprint of Simon & Schuster Children's Publishing Division.

To my husband and best friend, Scott,
who loves my cooking so much, he always wants more
—K. W.

For Tim and Noah, with love
—J. C.

Margaret K. McElderry Books
An imprint of Simon & Schuster Children's Publishing Division
1230 Avenue of the Americas
New York, New York 10020
Text copyright © 2003 by Karma Wilson
Illustrations copyright © 2003 by Jane Chapman

The text for this book is set in Adobe Caslon.
The illustrations for this book are rendered in acrylic paint.

ISBN 978-1-59961-489-2 (reinforced library bound edition)

Library of Congress Cataloging-in-Publication Data
This book was previously cataloged with the following information:

Wilson, Karma.
Bear wants more / Karma Wilson ; illustrations by Jane Chapman.
p. cm.
Summary: When spring comes, Bear wakes up very hungry and is treated to great food by his friends.
[1. Bears—Fiction. 2. Food—Fiction. 3. Animals—Fiction. 4. Stories in rhyme.] I. Chapman, Jane, 1970– ill. II. Title.
PZ8.3.W6976 Bew 2003
[E]—dc21
2001055889

When springtime comes,
in his warm winter den
a bear wakes up
very hungry and thin!

He waddles outside
and roots all around.
He digs and he paws
fresh shoots from the ground.

He nibbles on his lawn
till the last blade is gone.
But
the bear
wants more!

Mouse scampers by
with his acorn pail.
"Come along," Mouse squeaks,
"to Strawberry Vale!"

So up Mouse hops
onto Bear's big back.
They tromp through the woods
for a fresh fruit snack.

The berries grow sweet, and they eat, eat, EAT!

But
the bear
wants more!

The noon sun glows,
when along hops Hare.
"Good day, friend Mouse!
How do, friend Bear?"

"I'm HUNGRY!" roars Bear.
Hare says, "Follow me!
There's a fresh clover patch
by the cottonwood tree."

They nibble on their lunch,
with a crunch, crunch, crunch!

But
the bear
wants more!

Badger shuffles by
with his new fishin' pole.
"There's a fine fish feast
at the ol' fishin' hole."

They head to the pond
and they sit by the shore.
Bear catches fish, . . .

Meanwhile . . .
back at the big bear's den
wait Gopher and Mole
with Raven and Wren.

They bake honey cakes.
They decorate the lair.
It's a springtime party
for their good friend Bear!

Bear rubs at his tummy.
He smells something YUMMY . . .

and he still
wants
more!

Bear sniffs and he snuffles
as a sweet breeze blows.
He romps to his home.
He follows his nose.

His friends yell "SURPRISE!"
when he gets to his den.
But Bear is SO big . . .

. . . that he can't fit in!

Bear wails, "What luck! I am
STUCK, STUCK, STUCK . . .

in my own front door!"

Mouse squeaks, "Poor Bear.
He is wedged too tight."
Hare tugs, Raven pushes
with all of their might.

Badger gets a stick
and he pries SO hard . . .

. . . that Bear POPS out
and he lands in his yard!

Since Bear is SO WIDE, they party outside.

And he still wants more!

Bear opens presents;
he gobbles honey cakes.
He eats SO much
that his big tummy aches.

He snuggles in the grass
And he snores big snores.
He is full, full, full . . .

but . . .
his friends
want more!